The Steven Kellogg Connection

by Will C. Howell

FEARON TEACHER AIDS
Simon & Schuster Supplementary Education Group

SK

He just moved in. He is gentle, he is kind, he gives joy, he laughs and cries just like us, he helped me with my book, his name is Steven, and he says he'll be my friend. Can I keep him?

No, dear, you can't keep him. You must share him. But he may be your friend.

Thank you, Steven, for being my friend.

WH

Editor: Carol Williams
Copyeditor: Cynthia Seagren
Illustration: Gwen Connelly
Cover illustration: Steven Kellogg
Design: Diann Abbott

ISBN 0-8224-6452-7

Printed in the United States of America
1. 9 8 7 6 5 4

Contents

Introduction

The emphasis on "The Year of the Young Reader" (1989) and "International Literacy Year" (1990) has helped children's literature come of age. Research confirms that good reading and writing are best taught by using good books. And today, educators are fortunate to have a wide selection of excellent children's books to choose from.

The Steven Kellogg Connection is written for librarians and teachers who want to effectively use good literature in their classrooms. The lessons present art, math, creative writing, science, and social studies activities to accompany books by this one outstanding author. The variety of interdisciplinary activities and the whole-language instructional approach incorporated in the lessons will help you meet the diverse needs and interests of your students.

As students become familiar with various works by a single author, they develop an ability to analyze literary and artistic styles. The students can go to the library and select books written or illustrated by authors they feel as if they have actually met. "Connecting" with authors stimulates students to become involved in and enthusiastic about reading, writing, and learning. *The Steven Kellogg Connection* gives students the opportunity to meet an author/illustrator who has nearly one hundred books in print.

Lessons require minimal preparation, while resulting in maximum participation and learning. A brief synopsis of each book is included. Read the book aloud to the children and invite them to enjoy the illustrations before participating in the activities. Activities such as making word snakes, designing papier-mâché hot air balloons, counting by millions, and solving outrageous word problems will help you to enhance and reinforce your curriculum.

Meet Steven Kellogg

Steven Kellogg was born on October 26, 1941.

As a boy, he loved animals and he loved drawing. Steven would often sit between his sisters, holding a drawing pad on his lap. He would tell his sisters stories as he illustrated them before the girls' eyes. Steven Kellogg credits his grandmother for giving him a love for books and for teaching him to pay attention to the little things in life.

As a boy, Steven attempted to convince his mother to adopt many stray animals. His love for animals continues to this day. Steven actually has a Great Dane named Pinkerton. Rose, a character in the Pinkerton books, is based on the Kelloggs' cat, Secondhand Rose, who was found in the woods.

Steven took his love for animals, his attention to detail, and his interest in drawing with him to the Rhode Island School of Design and then to Italy for a year of study. Mr. Kellogg's first book, *The Orchard Rat,* was rejected. However, the illustrations in *The Orchard Rat* caught the eye of an editor and got Steven his first illustrating job, drawing the pictures for George Mendoza's *Gwot!* And many years later, *The Orchard Rat* was recreated and published as *The Orchard Cat.*

Steven Kellogg believes that a good children's book should be "a feast for the eyes, a feast for the ears, and a feast for the heart." He has given us many books that provide just such feasts!

A My Name Is

Reviving an old ball-bouncing rhyme, Jane Bayer has written a delightful text for Steven Kellogg's zany illustrations. This wonderful alphabet book is fun to read, sing from, and use as a pattern for original compositions.

Written by Jane Bayer
New York: Dial, 1984

Alice

ALPHABETIZING

Materials:

• lined paper
• pencils

Lesson Procedure

1. After reading the entire book for children to enjoy, read one page and have students write down all the words from that page beginning with the same letter.
2. Compile the list on the chalkboard to be sure that each student found all the words and that the words are spelled correctly.
3. Have each student alphabetize the list on their papers.

Alaska	anteater
Alex	ants
Alice	ape

4. Repeat the exercise, using other letter pages.
5. Provide paper and a copy of the book at an independent learning center. Encourage students to alphabetize the words from each page in their free time.

Taking It Further . . .

Create a class alphabet book, using the pattern in *A My Name Is Alice*. Each student can create one page, using the worksheet on page 9. Or, display an assortment of alphabet books and challenge students to create their own original books. Animals, cars, or space are possible themes. Students can create one page for each letter following their chosen theme.

Name _____

My name is _____ and
my husband's name is _____

We come from _____
and we sell _____

_____ is a _____. _____ is a _____.

A My Name Is Alice

Aster Aardvark's

Following the popularity of
A My Name Is Alice, Steven
Kellogg was encouraged by
friends to create another alphabet
book of his own, incorporating his
robust humor and illustrations.
The result is this book in which
Aster Aardvark gets into a series
of alliterative adventures. This col-
orful, comical collection will
inspire children to take a closer
look at letters and words.

New York:
William Morrow & Co., 1987

Alphabet Adventures

ALLITERATION

Materials:

•lined paper
•pencils

Lesson Procedure

1. Discuss alliteration after children listen to Aster's adventures. Copy some examples from the book on the chalkboard and underline the beginning letters or blends that sound alike.

   But <u>L</u>ana was so <u>l</u>ate not a <u>l</u>ick of <u>l</u>unch was <u>l</u>eft.

2. Have each student write an alliterative sentence or paragraph, using as many words as possible that begin with the first letter of his or her name.

   <u>C</u>arl <u>c</u>ouldn't <u>c</u>ut the <u>c</u>ake, so he <u>c</u>oncealed the <u>c</u>andy in his <u>c</u>oat.

Taking It Further . . .

Assign each student a different letter of the alphabet. Children describe new alliterative adventures for Aster Aardvark (or another main character chosen by the class) and add illustrations. Combine the pages together to make a class alphabet adventure book.

The Boy Who

It all started on an ordinary day to an ordinary boy. He discovered that he was being followed home by a hippopotamus. After several days, there were several hippopotami, and Robert's parents were not as delighted as Robert with a lawn full of hippos.

Written by Margaret Mahy
New York: Franklin Watts, Inc., 1975

Was Followed Home

✦ CREATIVE WRITING ✦

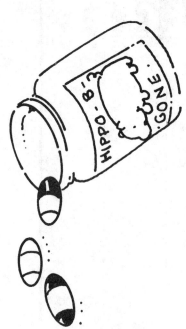

Materials:

• lined paper
• pencils
• pill bottles or film cans

Lesson Procedure

1. Discuss cause and effect and have students recall examples from the book.

   The abundance of hippos caused Robert's father to get help.
   The pill caused Robert to get sick.
   The pill caused Robert to be unattractive to hippos.
   The hippos leaving caused Robert's father to be happy.

2. Have students write about a new pill that will make the giraffes go away.
3. Guide students to include in their stories a description of the pill (shape, size, color, and taste), Robert's reaction to it, and the final effects of it.
4. When the stories are completed, students can fold them into narrow strips, roll them, and put them in pill bottles or film cans. Collect the pill bottles and redistribute them randomly. Students can open the bottles and read the stories aloud.

Taking It Further . . .

Students can write letters to Robert's father with helpful suggestions for getting rid of giraffes!

Barney

Barney is six. He wants to be eight. He also wants his dog, Snoozer, to talk, and he wants to drive a big, shiny car. When Miss Minerva Markle gives Barney three magic dandelions, his three wishes turn magic into mayhem.

Written by Carol Chapman
New York: Dial, 1988

Bipple's Magic Dandelions

❧ CREATIVE WRITING ☙

Materials:

- •lined paper
- •pencils

Lesson Procedure

1. After reading the book, have students think of other things that can be wished upon and list them on the chalkboard.

   wishbones
   throwing coins in a fountain
   first star in the evening sky

2. If possible, take students outside so that they can each pick three dandelions.
3. Have students write down their three wishes. Encourage students to include why they desire these wishes.

Taking It Further . . .

Have students trade papers and write possible outcomes if one or more of the wishes were to come true. For example, if one student wished for a swimming pool, another student can describe the outcome by saying that all the neighbors' dogs may come and swim in the pool every day.

Can I Keep

Arnold brings home a parade of animals, none of which he can keep, not even Ralph, who just moved in. Arnold's loneliness stirs his imagination to reach farther and farther, but Arnold's mother has it all under control.

New York: Dial, 1971

Him?

 **ANIMALS**

Materials:

- •worksheet on page 19
- •pencils
- •crayons or markers
- •encyclopedias and reference books

Lesson Procedure

1. On the chalkboard, make a list of the animals Arnold tried to bring home.
2. Discuss the reasons Arnold's mother gave for why these animals would not make good pets.
3. List additional animals and discuss reasons why they would not make good pets.
4. Using the worksheet, have students draw a picture of themselves in the top box and select one animal they would like to bring home to keep as a pet. Then have each student draw a picture of one of their parents in the bottom box and write reasons that parent might give for refusing to let the student keep the pet. Encourage students to consider the following questions:

What would it need to eat?
Where would it sleep?
How would it get exercise?

Does it have habits that might cause problems?
How would you keep it clean?

Students can use the reference materials to help them find factual information that supports their answers.

Taking It Further . . .

Invite children to creatively dramatize scenarios in which Arnold brings home a pet and his mother refuses to let him keep it. The student playing Arnold can choose an imaginary animal to present to and plead with his parent to let him keep it. The student playing the mother or father can give the excuses why Arnold cannot keep the animal as a pet. Point out how, in the story, Arnold's mother gave excuses that were directly related to the task she was doing at the moment Arnold was talking to her.

Can I Keep Him?

Name _____

I found this

_____

Can I keep him?

(Draw your parent here.)

(Draw yourself here.)

No, because . . .

_____
_____
_____
_____
_____
_____
_____
_____
_____
_____

Can I Keep Him?

Chicken Little

Steven Kellogg brings humor and his own brand of charm to his retelling of this popular tale about a panic-stricken chicken and her assorted followers. From the first sighting of the "Poulice" truck to the falling of the Sky Patrol to Chicken Little's final vindication, the book will keep readers rolling in rollicking fun.

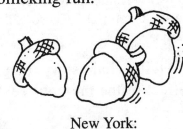

New York:
William Morrow & Co., 1985

CAUSE AND EFFECT

Materials:

- worksheets on pages 23–24
- pencils
- old magazines
- scissors
- glue

Lesson Procedure

1. Discuss how one event (cause) leads to another (effect) and how that event becomes the cause of another event. Have students recall examples from the story.

   (Cause) An acorn fell on Chicken Little's head.
   (Effect) Chicken Little thought the sky was falling. (Cause)
   (Effect) Chicken Little cried, "The sky is falling!" (Cause)
   (Effect) Henny Penny called the police.

2. Have students sit in a circle and tell a chain story. Each student adds one sentence to the story to emphasize the effect of the previous sentence.

   A plane hit a bird.
   The plane began to crash.
   The pilot jumped.
   He landed in a passing convertible.
   The convertible swerved.

3. Give each student a copy of both worksheets. Have students find magazine pictures to glue on the worksheets.
4. Have students exchange worksheets and write a cause or effect to go with the pictures.

Taking It Further . . .

Students can work in groups of 3–5 to create new chain-reaction stories. Have groups brainstorm, write rough drafts, edit, and publish a finished product.

Chicken Little

What Happened Next?

Glue a magazine picture in the box. Pass your paper to a friend. The friend can write what happened after the scene in the picture took place.

Cause:

Effect: _____

_____

_____

_____

_____

_____

_____

_____

Chicken Little

Why Did It Happen?

Glue a magazine picture in the box. Pass your paper to a friend. The friend can write what happened before the scene in the picture took place.

Cause: _____

_____

_____

_____

_____

_____

_____

_____

_____

Effect:

Come Here,

In contrast to some of the bold, robust humor and illustrations in some of his other books, Steven Kellogg has complemented the author's gentle text to create a warm little book. This is a simple, but powerful, story about a little girl and a cat who learn how to act toward each other.

Written by Joan L. Nødset
New York: Harper & Row,
1973

Cat

FRIENDSHIP

Materials:

- worksheet on page 27
- pencils

Lesson Procedure

1. Discuss ways the little girl won the cat's trust.

   She talked nicely.
   She moved slowly.
   She did not repeat things that had bothered the cat.

2. Discuss how the methods the little girl used to win the cat's trust can be used to build friendships.

   Talk nicely and be friendly to others.
   Be patient.
   Don't do things that bother others.

3. Pass out the worksheet. Have students write their own "friendship-building" ideas.

Taking It Further . . .

Students can write stories that tell about a time when a friend came to their rescue, or students can write stories telling when they were able to help out a friend in need.

Come Here, Cat

How to build a friendship:

1. _____
2. _____
3. _____
4. _____
5. _____
6. _____
7. _____
8. _____

Come Here, Cat

The Day

An ordinary class trip to the farm is made very extraordinary when Jimmy's pet boa constrictor sets off a chain of zany events.

Written by Trinka Hakes Noble
New York: Dial, 1980

Jimmy's Boa Ate the Wash

• VERBS •

Materials:

- •lined paper
- •drawing paper
- •pencils

Lesson Procedure

1. After reading the story, explain that a verb is an action word.
2. Read the story again very slowly and have students write each verb they hear on a sheet of lined paper.
3. After reading the story the second time, compile a list of verbs on the chalkboard from the students' lists.
4. Have each student fold a sheet of drawing paper into fourths. Students should select eight verbs from the chalkboard and write and illustrate one in each square on both sides of the paper.
5. After illustrating each verb, students can write a sentence using each word.

Taking It Further . . .

Each student can choose his or her favorite verb illustration, cut it out, and add it to a verb collage on a bulletin-board display. Or, write the verbs on 3" x 5" cards and have students take turns acting out each verb in a game of charades.

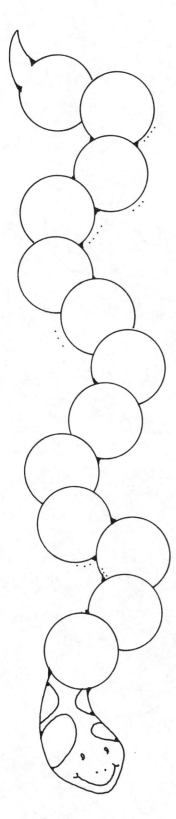

◄•● WORD STRUCTURE ●•►

Materials:

- worksheet on page 32
- pencils

Lesson Procedure

1. Copy this "word snake" on the chalkboard:

B O A T R A C T O R A L U N C H I C K E N S Q U A W K

A "word snake" is created by starting with one word and adding letters to create additional words. The words usually share ending or beginning letters.

2. Make a list on the chalkboard of all the words students can find in the "snake."

boa	tractor	chick
boat	actor	chickens
oat	oral	squaw
at	lunch	squawk

3. This is a good opportunity to discuss beginning and ending blends, prefixes, and suffixes.
4. Give each student a worksheet so that he or she can create an original "word snake."
5. Students can exchange papers to find all of the hidden words in the "snakes."

Taking It Further...

Encourage children to categorize the words they find in the "word snakes." Words can be grouped by vowel sounds, parts of speech, or word length.

Word Snake

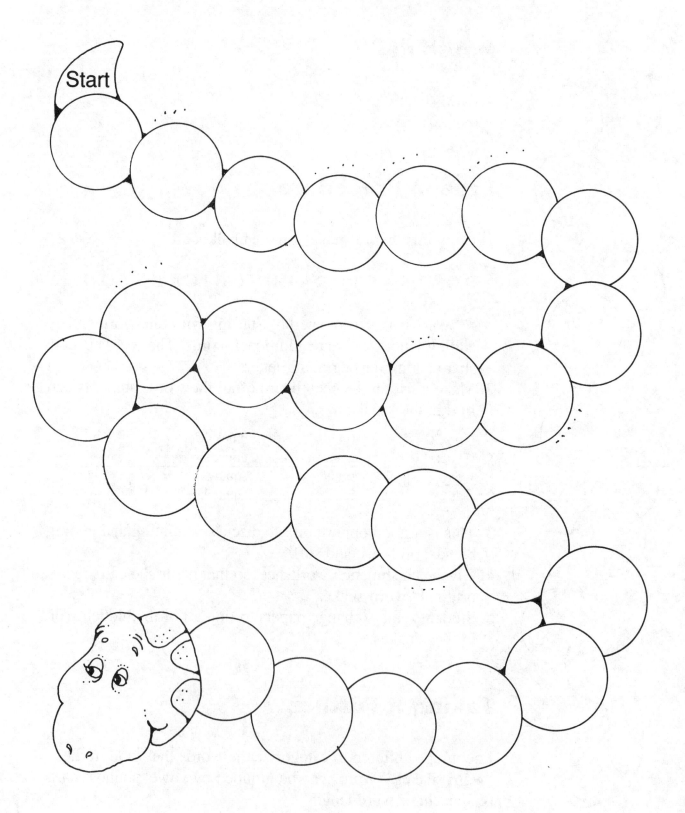

Start

The Steven Kellogg Connection © 1990 Fearon Teacher Aids

The Day Jimmy's Boa Ate the Wash

How Much Is a

Marvelosissimo the Mathematical Magician, with the help of Steven Kellogg's magical illustrations, takes children on a marvelous journey into large numbers. Millions, billions, and trillions are explored with imagination and calculation.

Written by David M. Schwartz
New York: Lothrop,
Lee & Shepard, 1985

Million?

ESTIMATING

Materials:

•worksheet on page 35
•pencils

Lesson Procedure

1. After reading the book, discuss the calculations by using the information the author has provided in the back of the book.
2. Present a new problem for students to calculate.

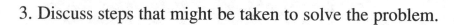
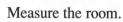

   If one million ants stood in a single-file line, how many times would their line cross the length of the classroom?

3. Discuss steps that might be taken to solve the problem.

   Measure the room.
   Find out the length of one ant.
   Determine how many ants it would take to cross the room once.
   Divide that number into one million.

4. Pass out a worksheet to each student. Encourage children to create and solve original word problems. Each student can enjoy creating a problem and then allowing a friend to solve it.
5. Bind the students' papers together to make a class book.

Taking It Further . . .

For further estimation practice, display a glass jar full of pennies, jelly beans, or marbles. Invite students to estimate the total number of items in the jar.

How Much Is a Million?

Name _____

How Much Is a Million?

Define your problem: _____

_____

_____

Solve the problem. Show your work step by step inside the whale.

Your conclusion: _____

If You Made a

Marvelosissimo the Mathematical Magician returns to take young readers on a fascinating journey into the world of money. Finally, a book that deals with money in an imaginative and creative way! Readers are challenged to think about how they could earn a penny, a dollar, or a lot of dollars. The author invites readers to picture what their pay would look like and how much it might weigh.

Written by David M. Schwartz
New York: Lothrop,
Lee & Shepard, 1989

Million

MONEY

Materials:

- lined paper
- pencils
- newspaper (ads and classified section)
- calculators

Lesson Procedure

1. Have students look through the classified ads to find jobs that interest them. Have each child make a list of jobs along with the salaries or hourly wages.
2. From the student lists, make a composite list of jobs on the chalkboard.
3. Each student can select one job and compute how long it would take to make a million dollars.

   Burger Cafe Chef earns $4.00 per hour
   $4.00 x 40 hours per week = $160.00 per week
   $160.00 x 52 weeks per year = $8,320.00 per year
   $1,000,000 divided by $8,320.00 = 120 years!
   Conclusion: You can't live long enough to make a million dollars selling hamburgers!

4. Some students may want to see how long it would take to make a million dollars through investments in savings certificates or stocks.

Taking It Further . . .

Encourage students to browse through the newspaper ads and make lists of things they would buy with a million dollars. Their lists may include clothing, games, real estate, cars, and trips.

If You Made a Million

The Island of

A delightful adventure story, complete with villains, a shipwreck, and, of course, a happy ending.

New York: Dial, 1973

the Skog

MAPPING

Materials:

- map on page 41
- pencils

Lesson Procedure

1. After reading the story, have children speculate where the mice may have sailed.
2. Give each student a copy of the world map. Have students label the continents and locate where they live.
3. Discuss facts from the book that give clues where the mice may have begun their journey.

> They left from a wharf. (This fact indicates they were on the coast.)
> A policeman holding a club is in the background. (This may indicate the wharf was in the United States or England.)
> The mice met under a bowling alley. (The United States has many bowling alleys.)

4. Discuss facts from the book that give clues where the mice may have sailed.

> They sailed into the sunrise. (This clue suggests they were sailing east.)
> They sailed into ice. (This indicates they were sailing north.)
> On the island, the sun was shining, plants were growing, and the mice were not huddled togther to keep warm. (These clues indicate that the island had a tropical or warm climate.)

5. See if children can come to any reasonable conclusions about the path of the sailing adventure. Remind students that Steven Kellogg's home is on the east coast of the United States in Connecticut. Perhaps the author had his home in mind as he charted the sailing path for the mice.

Taking It Further . . .

Have students draw maps of the island where the mice landed. Encourage them to include specific items mentioned in the book, such as Skog's home, Bouncer's home, a water source, and gardens.

The Island of the Skog

World Map

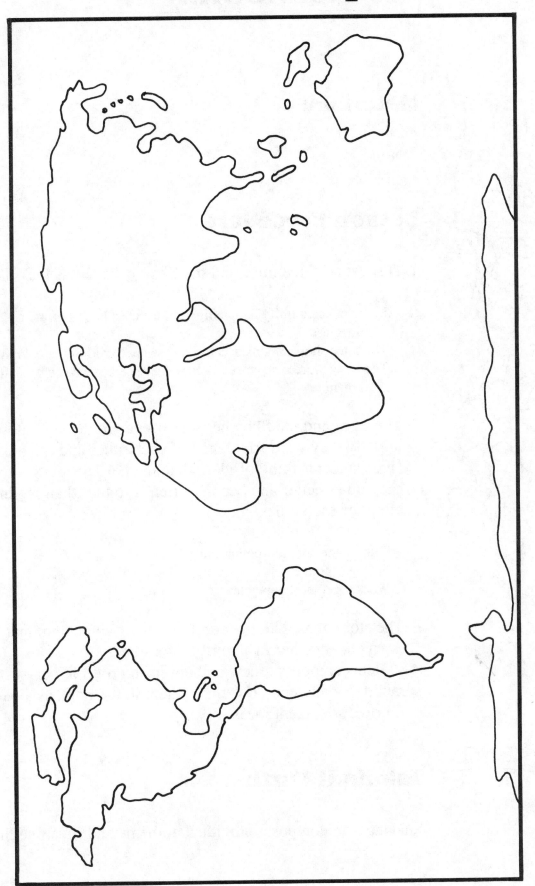

The Island of the Skog

FRIENDSHIP

Materials:

None

Lesson Procedure

1. Discuss why the mice and the Skog behaved as they did.

   Bouncer acted huffy and belligerent because he felt afraid and
       powerless.
   The mice shot cannons because they were afraid of the unknown.
   The Skog wore a disguise to scare the mice because he was afraid
       of them.

2. The mice and the Skog become friends in the end, although
   initially they were frightened of each other and the unknown.
   Have students think of ideas that can help people get to know
   each other better and become friends, rather than feeling
   afraid of each other.

   Talk to one another (communicate)
   Help each other
   Work together (cooperate)

3. The story ends with the construction of an anthem that binds
   everyone together in a spirit of comradery. As a class, have
   students compose a new anthem for a group of bears, snakes,
   rabbits, or students. Use the anthem in the book as a pattern to
   follow for content ideas.

Taking It Further . . .

Students can compose individual anthems and illustrate them.

Iva Dunnit

Steven Kellogg's wild illustrations bring this tall tale of the prairie to life. Children will enjoy the courage, loyalty, and resourcefulness of Carol Purdy's heroine and her six children.

Written by Carol Purdy
New York: Dial, 1985

and the Big Wind

PIONEER HISTORY

Materials:

- worksheet on page 45
- pencils
- resource material on pioneer life

Lesson Procedure

1. After reading the story, discuss with the students the things Iva Dunnit would need to set up her home on the prairie.
2. Divide the class into research groups of 4–6 students. Each group should find out the size of a typical covered wagon and what the load limit was.
3. Have the students list items on the worksheet that Iva would have to take with her in the covered wagon as she set off to make a home on the prairie.
4. Have students estimate the weight of each item or how much room it would occupy in the wagon to determine how many supplies could be taken. In order to remain within the wagon's load limit, luxury items may need to be eliminated.
5. Conclude the activity by having groups compare their lists.

Taking It Further . . .

Students can write stories entitled "The Big Wind Comes to School." Or, guide the class in researching and designing a covered wagon model.

Iva Dunnit and the Big Wind

Necessary supplies that Iva Dunnit could fit in her covered wagon:

Wagon size: _____

Load limit: _____

Jimmy's Boa

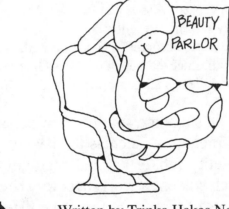

Children will enjoy more hilarious adventures of Jimmy's boa. The intrepid boa starts off another raucous chain of events, this time at a garden club.

BEAUTY PARLOR

Written by Trinka Hakes Noble
New York: Dial, 1984

Bounces Back

❧• CREATIVE WRITING •❧

Materials:

- worksheet on page 49
- pencils

Lesson Procedure

1. Discuss a series of cause-and-effect events from the story.

   The boa caused Miss Ivy to faint.
   Miss Ivy hit Miss Peachtree.
   Miss Peachtree dropped her poodle in the punch.
   The poodle sneezed punch on Miss Greenleaf.
   Miss Greenleaf's alligator purse caught Mrs. Rosebud's wig.

2. Hand each student a small slip of paper with the name of a place written on it, such as the beauty parlor, grocery store, zoo, athletic club, or baseball stadium.
3. Give each student a worksheet to write about the new adventures of the boa at the place listed on the small slip of paper.

Taking It Further . . .

Have students use magazines to cut out pictures of settings for boa stories. Read the description of *Jimmy's Boa Bounces Back* on the inside of the book jacket. Then have students glue their pictures on notebook paper and write short, descriptive "reviews."

Name _____

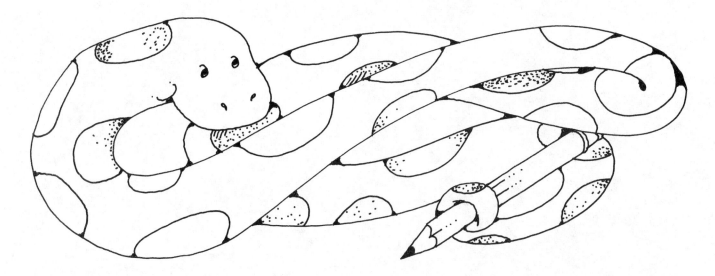

You won't believe what happened the day Jimmy's boa showed up at

_____

_____

_____

_____

_____

_____

_____

_____

_____

_____

_____

_____

_____

_____

_____

_____

Johnny

Steven Kellogg's retelling of the legend of John Chapman is filled with color, humor, and celebration. His characters seem to leap from the pages to draw young and old alike through the enchanting narrative.

New York:
William Morrow & Co., 1988

Appleseed

❧ • WRITING SKILLS • ❧

Materials:

• 3" x 5" cards
• pencils

Lesson Procedure

1. Discuss and make a list on the chalkboard of things that can be made from apples.

    applesauce
    apple pie
    apple fritters
    apple cider
    apple butter

2. Have each child choose one apple treat from the chalkboard and write a recipe for making it. Remind students of the importance of clearly written directions that follow a step-by-step progression.
3. Keep the recipes in a file box for students to enjoy looking at during their free time.

Taking It Further . . .

Encourage students to bring in actual recipes that use apples as a major ingredient. Compare the actual recipes with the ones the students wrote. Or encourage students to research various types of apples.

Johnny Appleseed

❧• SHARING IDEAS •❧

Materials:

- worksheet on page 54
- 9" x 12" red construction paper
- pencils
- scissors
- glue

Lesson Procedure

1. Discuss Johnny Appleseed's "mission" (to clear land, plant orchards, and provide apples for the settlers). Besides providing apples, Johnny demonstrated his respect for living things and shared his philosophy, "You get out of life what you put into it." Point out to the students that the things Johnny "shared" fit into three categories:

   a thing—apple trees
   an idea—respect for living things
   a proverb—"You get out of life what you put into it."

2. Encourage students to think about a thing, an idea, and a proverb that they would like to "share" with the world.
3. Give students the worksheet to write down their ideas.
4. Students can cut the apple pieces apart and glue them in an apple shape on red construction paper.

Taking It Further . . .

Brainstorm some ways students can share with each other (share a lunch item, a book, a game, or ball). Invite students to choose a sharing idea, put it into practice, and tell about it the next day.

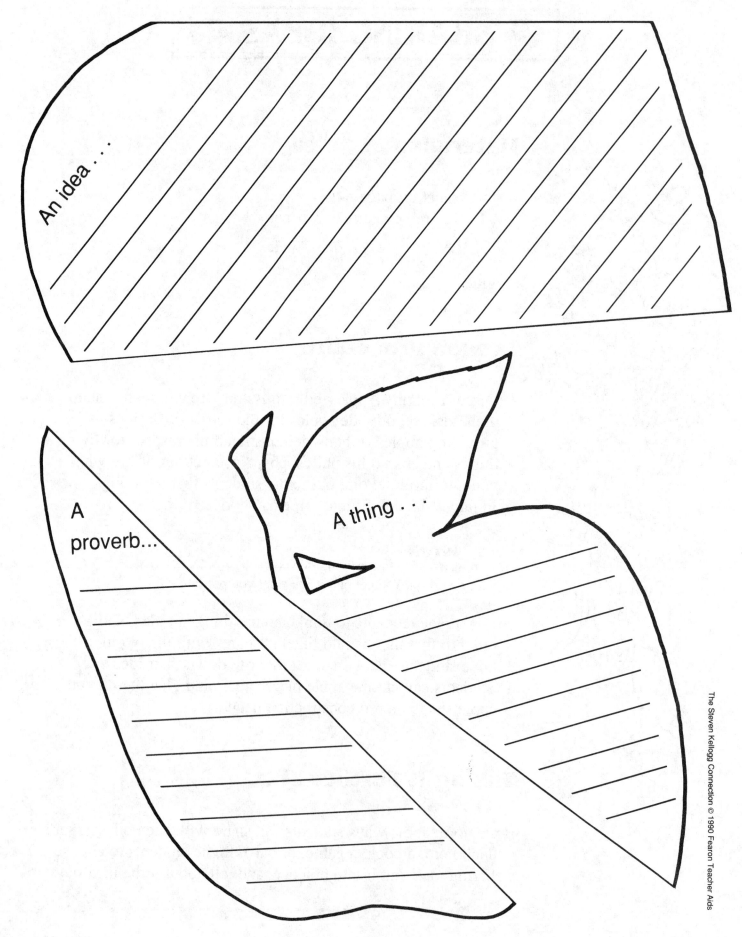

An idea . . .

A proverb...

A thing . . .

Johnny Appleseed

Leo, Zack, and

Emmie is the new girl in Room 208, and Leo and Zack think she's super until their own friendship seems threatened.

Written by Amy Ehrlich
New York: Dial, 1981

Emmie

Materials:

•3" x 5" cards

Lesson Procedure

1. After reading the book, discuss some of the dynamics of a friendship involving three people: sometimes, one person gets left out.
2. Review the rules of the card game Old Maid. Point out that two matching cards make a pair and the person left with the card that has no match (Old Maid) is left out. Discuss the similarities between this game and the friendship between the threesome—Leo, Zack, and Emmie.
3. Choose a skill that needs reinforcing, such as short vowels. Have students think of as many short-vowel word pairs as possible and list them on the chalkboard.

    jungle/tumble
    ask/bath

4. Make a set of Old Maid cards from the list. Print one word on each card until you have made 15–20 word pairs. Make three more cards by writing "Leo," "Zack," or "Emmie" on each card. These three cards are wild cards. Two of them make a pair and the one that is left out is the Old Maid card.
5. Encourage groups of 3–5 students to play together. Deal all of the cards out to students. The students sit in a circle and take turns drawing cards from each other. Each time a match is made, the student with the match puts the word pair on the table. The game ends when one student has a single, unmatched card.

Taking It Further . . .

Make other Old Maid card games by using contractions, long vowels, prefixes, suffixes, consonant blends, or silent letters.

Leo, Zack, and

With warmth and humor, Amy Ehrlich and Steven Kellogg bring back the three friends. This time the lively threesome deal with snow, Santa Claus, the chicken pox, and Valentine's Day.

Written by Amy Ehrlich
New York: Dial, 1987

Emmie
Together Again

HEALTH

Materials:

- •lined paper
- •pencils
- •encyclopedias
- •health reference books

Lesson Procedure

1. After reading the story, discuss and list diseases on the chalkboard.

   chicken pox
   measles
   cold
   flu

2. Discuss the meaning of the words *symptom, prevention,* and *cure*.
3. In groups of 2–4, have students choose a disease and research it, using the reference materials.
4. Instruct each group to include the following information in their report:

   1. How the disease is "caught"
   2. Symptoms
   3. Cure and care
   4. Prevention and control
   5. History

Taking It Further . . .

Provide students with black construction paper, white paint, and cotton swabs. Students can make snow pictures by using the cotton swabs to dab white paint on the black paper. Other details can be added with a paintbrush or by adding a collage of cutout shapes.

Leo, Zack, and Emmie Together Again

Millicent the

Oliver and Ronald learn a lesson on "being your own bear" from Millicent, the circus bear.

Written by Alice Bach
New York: Harper & Row, 1978

Magnificent

VOCABULARY

Materials:

- •lined paper
- •pencils
- •dictionaries

Lesson Procedure

1. Use the following list of words to play "Dictionary Bluff" with the class:

canter	sleight (of hand)	defiant
amble	momentum	spangle
gape	compressed (air)	stupefy
illusion	hurtle	bellow

2. Write one word from the list on the chalkboard and have each student write a made-up definition while you write the real definition on a small piece of paper.
3. Select three student definition "bluffs" and the actual definition, assign each definition a number, and read them aloud to the class.
4. Students try to distinguish the real definition from the "bluffs" by writing down the number of the definition they think is the correct one.
5. Continue the same process with other words from the chalkboard list.
6. When the game is over, have students look up the correct definitions in the dictionaries and tally their scores. They receive one point for each correct guess.
7. Students can also earn points for each person who guesses their "bluff" as the correct definition.

Taking It Further . . .

Invite students to use the new words in original sentences to reinforce the correct definitions.

Millicent the Magnificent

❖ SELF-AWARENESS ❖

Materials:

- •Oliver Award on page 62
- •lined paper
- •pencils

Lesson Procedure

1. Encourage students to discuss their talents.
2. Make a list on the chalkboard of talents or skills that students would like to develop.
3. Guide students to set realistic goals for learning a new skill. Students can learn to play chess, make spaghetti, do some stitchery, build a model, or stand on their heads.
4. Have students write down their goals. Keep the papers in a safe place to refer to after a predetermined amount of time to see if the goals have been accomplished.
5. Present each student who accomplishes the goal with an Oliver Award!

Taking It Further . . .

Help students who did not reach their goals to determine why, set a more realistic goal, and try again.

Oliver Award

presented to

_____

Accomplishment

_____

_____

_____

_____

_____

Signed _____

Oliver Award

presented to

_____

Accomplishment

_____

_____

_____

_____

_____

Signed _____

The Steven Kellogg Connection © 1990 Fearon Teacher Aids

Molly Moves

Ten rabbits living in one house is nine rabbits too many for Molly. Children with brothers and sisters will be rooting for Molly as she strikes out for independence.

Written by Susan Pearson
New York: Dial, 1979

Out

FAMILY RELATIONSHIPS

Materials:

- •worksheet on page 66
- •pencils

Lesson Procedure

1. Discuss the advantages and disadvantages of having brothers and sisters. List student responses on the chalkboard.

2. Discuss Molly's ideas for dealing with the problems she had with her brothers and sisters.

   She took Gregory fishing.
   She took Mary berry picking.
   She took John to the meadow.
   She moved out.

3. Discuss Molly's ideas for dealing with her new problem of loneliness.

   She planted a garden.
   She went for a swim.
   She had a cookout.

4. Help students begin generating constructive ideas to deal with problems they have with brothers and sisters.

   Find a quiet place.
   Think of helpful things to do for brothers and sisters.
   Join a club.

5. Give students the worksheet to list the problems they have with their brothers and sisters and to write down possible solutions. Encourage students who have no brothers and sisters to write about problems with other family members or friends.

Taking It Further . . .

Invite each student to design a poster advertising one important advantage of having a brother, sister, or close friend.

Name _____

Molly Moves On

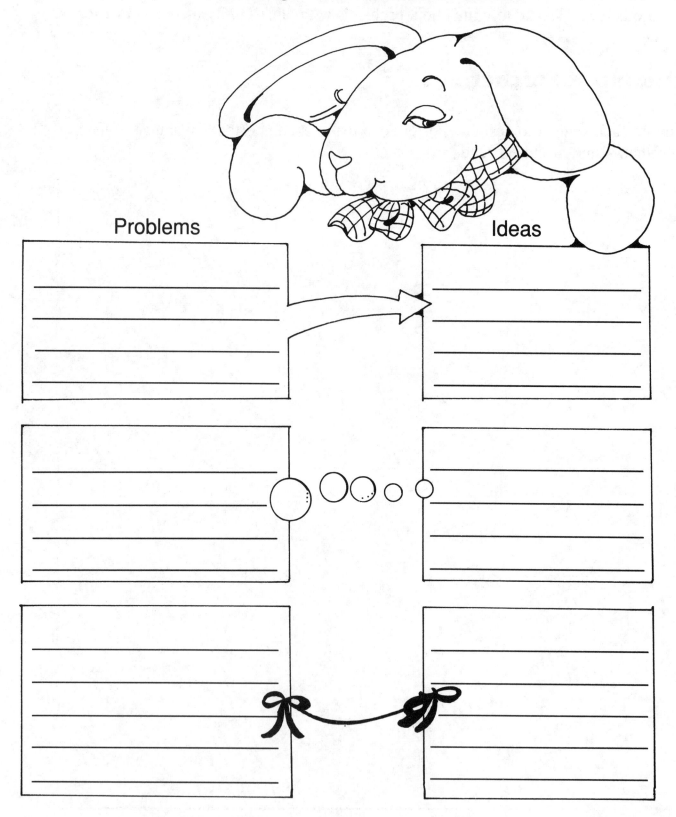

Problems

Ideas

The Steven Kellogg Connection © 1990 Fearon Teacher Aids

Molly Moves Out

Much

Henry wants to be bigger than his brother Martin. He tries stretching himself, watering himself, and eating an entire bagful of apples, all to no avail. His final solution is the most ingenious and effective.

New York: Dial, 1976

Bigger Than Martin

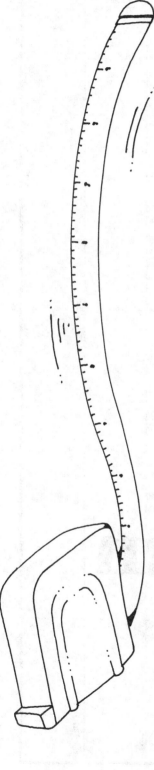

❧ FAMILY RELATIONSHIPS ❧

Materials:

- poster board
- markers
- lined paper
- pencils

Lesson Procedure

1. Discuss with the class the disadvantages of being a little brother or sister.
2. Discuss the advantages of having a big brother or sister.
3. Encourage students to share their reactions to the problem of Martin's little brother.
4. Plan a Brother/Sister Convention. Students can choose to join either the Big Brother/Sister Club or the Little Brother/Sister Club. Each group can make posters and write speeches defending their right to air their grievances.

    Big brothers get stuck baby-sitting.
    Little sisters have to wear hand-me-down clothes.
    Big sisters get to stay up late.
    Little brothers don't have to do as much work.

Taking It Further. . .

The book does not directly tell the name of Martin's little brother. See if students can figure out his name. Hint: Look at the picture that shows the height measurements of the two boys on the bathroom wall. Read *If I Had* by Mercer Mayer. New York: Dial, 1968.

The Mysterious

Louis receives an unusual tadpole from his Uncle McAlister in Scotland, and a typical Kellogg chain of events follows.

New York: Dial, 1977

Tadpole

CREATIVE WRITING

Materials:

•worksheet on page 71
•pencils

Lesson Procedure

1. Read the book to the children, but be sure not to let them see the last page, which shows the egg Louis received for his next birthday hatching.
2. Discuss with the students what they think may hatch out of this egg.
3. Pass out the worksheet and have students write about what hatches out of the egg and the events that may follow.

Taking It Further . . .

Students can draw a picture of what hatched out of the birthday egg or a picture of other gifts Louis may have received.

The Mysterious Tadpole

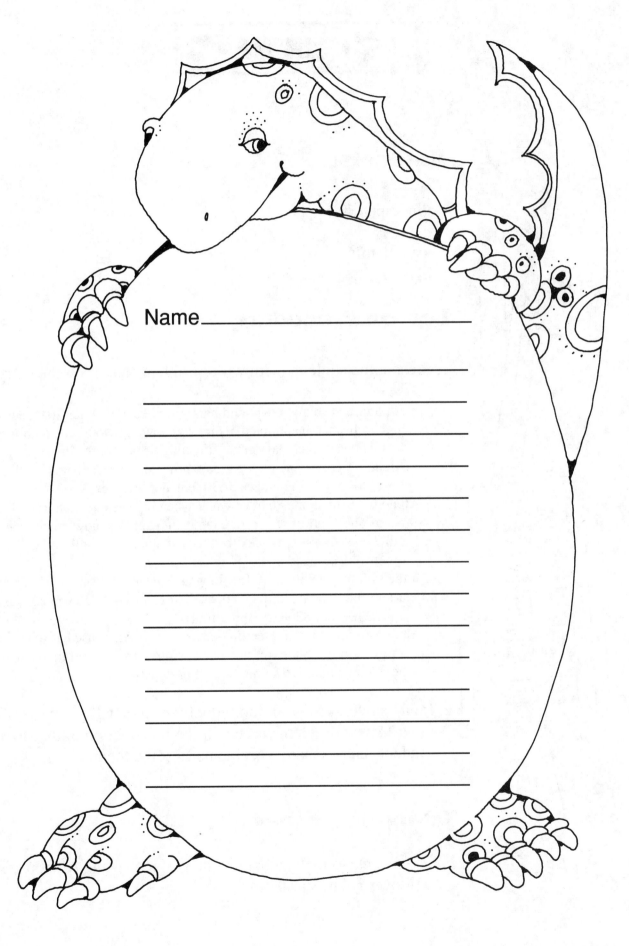

Name_____

_____

_____

_____

_____

_____

_____

_____

_____

_____

_____

_____

The Mysterious Tadpole

Materials:

- lined paper
- pencils
- calculators

Lesson Procedure

1. Present the students with word problems based on the story.

   If Alphonse ate a quarter-pound hamburger each day the first week and each week he doubled his intake, how big would the hamburger be that he ate each day on the fifteenth week? (4,096 lbs.)

   If Alphonse grows one inch per day, how long will he be on Louis' next birthday? (365 inches or 30 feet and 5 inches)

   Alphonse needed one quart of water when he was one inch long. If he needs one quart of water for each inch he grows, how much water will he need on Louis' next birthday in quarts? In gallons? (365 quarts or 91 $\frac{1}{4}$ gallons)

   If the swimming pool is 50 feet long and the swim team swims 23 laps after school, how many feet does the team swim? How many yards? (1,150 feet or 383 yards and 1 foot)

   Alphonse can swim 100 feet in one minute. If Alphonse has to dive 275 feet to reach the treasure chest and return 275 feet to the boat, how long would it take him? (5 $\frac{1}{2}$ minutes)

2. Invite students to work individually or in small groups of 2–3 to write new problems based on the information in the story.
3. Students can exchange problems to solve them.

Taking It Further . . .

Invite students to make a bar or line graph charting Alphonse's growth over a ten-year period.

RESEARCH

Materials:

- •worksheet on page 74
- •lined paper
- •pencils
- •3" x 5" cards
- •encyclopedias and other reference material

Lesson Procedure

1. Discuss things that are characteristic of Scotland, such as the Loch Ness monster or bagpipes.
2. Discuss things that are characteristic of other countries.

Australia—kangaroo
Holland—wooden shoes

Ireland—shamrock
Japan—chopsticks

Mexico—piñata

3. Pass out a 3" x 5" card with the name of a country written on it to each student.

Argentina	Ethiopia	Japan	Peru	Turkey
Australia	Egypt	Kenya	Poland	Uganda
Barbados	France	Mexico	Russia	Uruguay
Burundi	West Germany	Netherlands	Spain	Venezuela
China	Greece	New Zealand	Sweden	Yugoslavia
Cuba	India	Nigeria	Switzerland	Zaire
Denmark	Ireland	Norway	Thailand	Zimbabwe

4. After doing research, have each student list five possible gifts that could be sent from the country written on the 3" x 5" card. Encourage students to choose gifts that are unique to that particular country.
5. Using the worksheet, have each student illustrate and write about one of the items from the list.

Taking It Further . . .

Invite students to learn a word or phrase in the native language of their assigned country and share it with the class.

The Mysterious Tadpole

Name _____

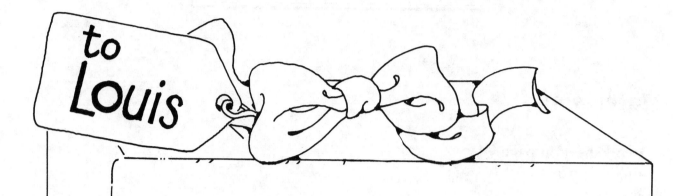

Dear Louis,

This is a_____ .
It is from_____ . I was
going to send you a _____ ,
_____ , _____ ,
or a _____ , but I
decided on the enclosed because _____
_____
_____
_____
_____
_____

Love,
Uncle X

The Mysterious Tadpole

The Mystery

Brian, Ellis, Joan, and Mrs. Wilkins design a plan to recover their pumpkin from Mr. Klug. Revenge is sweet, and in the end everyone is happy.

New York: Dial, 1980

of the Flying Orange Pumpkin

CREATIVE WRITING

Materials:

- worksheet on page 77
- lined paper
- pencils

Lesson Procedure

1. Pass out a worksheet to each student.
2. In the first box, students design pumpkin seed packets.
3. In the second box, students write directions for planting seeds.
4. On the bottom half of the worksheet, students write about what will happen when the seeds begin to grow.

Taking It Further . . .

Have students choose one of the following ideas to write about:

- Describe what the Patterson Pumpkin Club will do next year.
- Tell what Mr. Klug will do next.
- Write a recipe for making pumpkin pie.
- Write directions for making a jack-o'-lantern.
- Explain why Mr. Bramble had to move away.

Or, students can design jack-o'-lanterns, using orange construction paper.

76   *The Mystery of the Flying Orange Pumpkin*

Magic Pumpkin Seeds

How to Plant

1. _____

2. _____

3. _____

4. _____

What will happpen when the seeds begin to grow?

_____

_____

_____

_____

_____

_____

_____

_____

_____

FRIENDSHIP

Materials:

- worksheet on page 79
- pencils

Lesson Procedure

1. Discuss "tricks" or "treats" of friendship. Make a list on the chalkboard as children recall the friendly and unfriendly actions of the characters in the story.

Tricks (<u>unfriendly</u>)	Treats (<u>friendly</u>)
Mr. Klug wouldn't let Joan water the pumpkin.	Mr. Bramble let the children use his garden.

2. Give several examples of "tricks" (unfriendly actions) that children might play on each other and have children think of a "treat" (friendly response).

   Some children call others names (trick), while some children compliment others (treat). Some children take things without asking (trick), while some children offer to share their things with others (treat).

3. Pass out the worksheet and have children write their own examples of "tricks" or "treats" of friendship.

Taking It Further . . .

Create a "Tricks or Treats" bulletin board. List classroom behavior without mentioning any names.

<u>Tricks</u>	<u>Treats</u>
A lot of litter was on the floor today.	Someone cleaned up the floor for us today.

The Mystery of the Flying Orange Pumpkin

Tricks

Treats

The Mystery of the Flying Orange Pumpkin

The Mystery

Complete with a villain and a heroine, this humorous mystery solves a big problem in a little boy's life.

New York: Dial, 1978

of the Magic Green Ball

ART

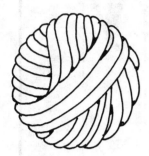

Materials:

•parent letter on page 83

Lesson Procedure

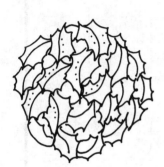

1. Discuss other ways Peggy and Timmy could have made a fake magic green ball.
2. Tell the students that you are going to have a Magic Green Ball Look Alike Contest. Send home a copy of the parent letter with each child. Encourage students to think of creative plans and to design unique fake magic green balls at home (or the materials can be brought to school).
3. Award prizes for the most creative ball, the ball made with the most unusual material, the greenest ball, and the ball that looks most like Timmy's.

Taking It Further . . .

Students can write step-by-step directions for making fake magic green balls.

The Mystery of the Magic Green Ball

Date _____

Dear Parent,

We have just finished reading *The Mystery of the Magic Green Ball* by Steven Kellogg. In the story, a mystery gypsy uses a green ball that belongs to Timmy as her magic ball. Peggy and Timmy paint a grapefruit green to create a fake green ball and exchange it for Timmy's real ball when the gypsy isn't looking.

   Our class is going to have a Magic Green Ball Look Alike Contest. Each student has one week to create a fake green ball. Any material may be used with your approval. Awards will be presented in the following categories:

   •most creative
   •most unusual material
   •greenest
   •most closely resembling Timmy's

The deadline for entries is _____

Thank you for your help in this project.

Sincerely,

☙• LITERATURE •☙

PLOT
1. Beginning
2. Middle
3. End

CHARACTERS

STYLE

SETTING

THEME

Materials:

None

Lesson Procedure

1. Make a list on the chalkboard of the elements for a good story.

Plot—action with a definite beginning, middle, and end. A problem should be presented in the beginning, struggled with in the middle, and resolved in the end.

Characters—hero (protagonist) and villain (antagonist)

Style—the way a story is told (words and pictures)

Setting—where and when the story takes place

Theme—the message of the story (friendship, courage, etc.)

2. Discuss these elements as they relate to the story.

PLOT: Beginning—Timmy loses his ball.
Middle—Sara Bianco has the ball.
End—Timmy and Peggy recover the ball.
CHARACTERS: Timmy is the main character.
Sara is the villain (antagonist).
Peggy is the heroine because she comes to the rescue.
STYLE: Steven Kellogg uses gentle humor in his writing and in the illustrations.
SETTING: Children will easily identify with the ordinary neighborhood setting.
THEME: The theme could be friendship, problem solving, or overcoming evil with good.

Taking It Further . . .

Encourage students to rewrite Steven Kellogg's story by changing one of the five elements. For example, the story could be rewritten with new characters or a new setting.

The Mystery of the Magic Green Ball

The Mystery

Steven Kellogg creates another charming, high-spirited
minute-mystery for the very
young. This little book is big on
imagination, charm, and humor.

New York: Dial, 1974

of the Missing
Red Mitten

❧ • CREATIVE THINKING • ❧

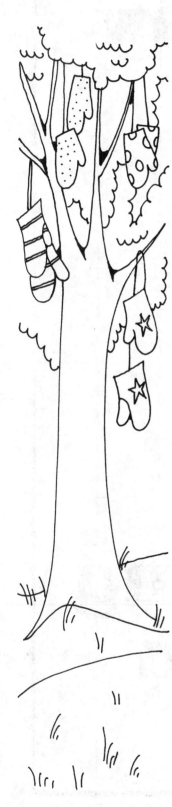

Materials:

- lined paper
- pencils
- red construction paper
- scissors
- glue

Lesson Procedure

1. Have children recall Annie's thoughts about the ways her lost mitten could be used.

   sleeping bag for mice
   hat for a baby hawk
   a seed to grow a "mitten" tree
   a snowman's heart

2. Give each child a sheet of lined paper and set the timer for ten minutes. Have students list as many new uses as they can think of for a red mitten.
3. Reset the timer for an additional five minutes and invite students to share their ideas in groups of 4–6.
4. Each student can draw and cut out a large mitten from red construction paper and glue their ideas in the center.
5. This activity can be done orally with very young children. Make a list of ideas on the chalkboard. Or, younger students can sketch their ideas rather than write them.

Taking It Further . . .

Students can bring their favorite mittens to school. Label the mittens with the students' names and hang them on a clothesline or a "mitten tree."

The Mystery of the Missing Red Mitten

Paul Bunyan

Kellogg's illustrations add warmth and humor to some of Paul's wildest adventures. Readers will delight in following Paul across the continent and cheering his heroic deeds.

New York:
William Morrow & Co., 1984

CREATIVE WRITING

Materials:

- worksheet on page 89
- lined paper
- pencils
- other versions of Paul Bunyan

Lesson Procedure

1. After reading Steven Kellogg's version of Paul Bunyan, read other versions and have students compare the similarities and differences.
2. Explain that a tall tale is often told to explain a natural phenomenon as well as to pass time and provide entertainment.
3. List the examples of the origins of natural phenomena explained in the tall tale about Paul Bunyan.

   Great Lakes
   St. Lawrence River
   Rocky Mountains
   Great Plains
   Grand Canyon

4. Have students think of other natural wonders, such as the Mississippi River, Yosemite Falls, Everglades, Mt. St. Helens, Carlsbad Caverns. List them on the chalkboard.
5. Pass out the worksheet to students. Have them select a natural wonder and write a tall tale to explain its origin.

Taking It Further . . .

Display collections of folk tales that represent a variety of ethnic origins (Native American, African, Asian). Encourage students to read them and look for similarities and to make comparisons.

Name _____

Paul Bunyan and _____

Write a tall tale to explain the origin of a natural wonder.

_____
_____
_____
_____
_____
_____
_____
_____
_____
_____
_____
_____
_____
_____
_____
_____
_____
_____

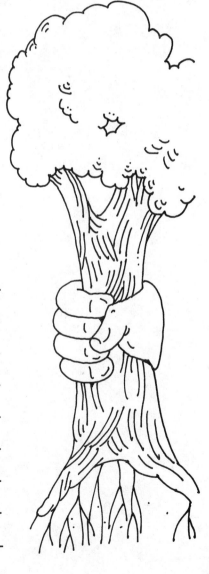

Paul Bunyan

Pecos Bill

Steven Kellogg brings another American folk hero to life with outrageous humor and wild energy. Pecos Bill arrives in Texas as an infant and grows up to be the larger-than-life hero of the West. He takes on a giant rattlesnake, longhorn cattle, a lightning-fast stallion, and finally Slewfoot Sue.

New York:
William Morrow & Co.,1986

SEQUENCING

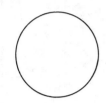

Materials:

•worksheet on page 93
•pencils

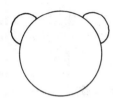

Lesson Procedure

1. Point out the bears in the illustrations on the endpapers of the book. Speculate why Steven Kellogg chose to draw bears. Discuss other animals that are pictured in the story.
2. Show students how to draw a simple bear face, using the step-by-step illustrations on the worksheet.
3. Give each student a worksheet. Have students write directions, using complete sentences, to describe how to draw each of the six steps.

Taking It Further . . .

Students can choose other animals and make up simple steps for drawing them, including pictures and complete sentences. Or, have students compare different versions of Pecos Bill.

Pecos Bill

Name _____

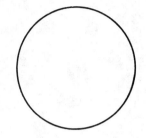

1.

2.

3.

4.

5.

6.

1. _____

_____

2. _____

_____

3. _____

_____

4. _____

_____

5. _____

_____

6. _____

_____

Pecos Bill

Pinkerton,

Everyone can identify with the hilarious antics of a Great Dane who goes to obedience school. Commands are confused and messages mixed-up, until the dog gets his masters trained. Pinkerton is a lovable disaster on four big feet.

New York: Dial, 1979

Behave!

VERBS

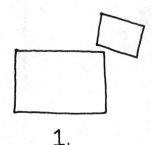

1.

Materials:

• worksheet on page 97
• pencils

Lesson Procedure

1. After reading the book, pass out the worksheet and have students make lists of tricks you can teach a dog.

> Come
> Fetch
> Attack (the burglar)
> Play dead
> Roll over

2. Have students underline the verbs in the list of tricks and use each verb in an original sentence.

> I told my brother to <u>come</u> home.
> My sister <u>fetched</u> the mail.

3. Have students write a synonym for each verb.

> come—return
> fetch—bring
> attack—charge
> play dead—act dead
> roll—tumble

3.

Taking It Further . . .

Teach the students to draw simple box-shaped Pinkertons. After mastering the technique, students can draw Pinkertons to illustrate their list of dog tricks.

Pinkerton, Behave!

Dog Tricks

Make a list of tricks that you can teach a dog.

_____
_____
_____
_____
_____
_____
_____
_____

Underline each verb (action word) in the list of tricks above. Use each underlined verb in a sentence below.

_____
_____
_____
_____
_____
_____
_____
_____

On the back of your paper, write a synonym for each verb.

The Steven Kellogg Connection © 1990 Fearon Teacher Aids

Pinkerton, Behave!

❧ • NOUNS AND ADJECTIVES • ❧

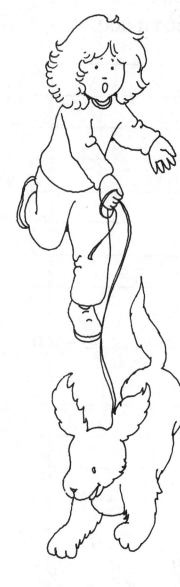

Materials:

•lined paper
•pencils

Lesson Procedure

1. After reading the story, have each student make a list of
   supplies that might be needed in a dog obedience school,
   such as rope, newspaper, or a clipboard.
2. Explain to the students that their lists of supplies are lists of
   nouns. Have students write an adjective to describe each
   noun in the supply list.
3. Encourage students to use the adjective-noun pairs in original
   sentences.

   The boat was tied to the dock with <u>strong rope</u>.

Taking It Further . . .

Read *A Rose for Pinkerton*.

Prehistoric

Pinkerton is back! This time the lovable Great Dane is teething. The fun begins when Pinkerton visits the museum and finds some bones just his size.

New York: Dial, 1987

Pinkerton

☙• CREATIVE WRITING •❧

Materials:

• lined paper
• pencils

Lesson Procedure

1. Discuss the statement in the book, "Pinkerton's great, great, great . . . grandmother may have been a stegosaurus." Point out how we have some of the same characteristics, likes and dislikes, and physical attributes as our ancestors.
2. Have children think about ways they are like their ancestors (grandparents or other relatives). Have each student choose one ancestor they admire and respect and make a list of the positive characteristics or attributes of that ancestor.
3. Give students lined paper to write paragraphs relating one of the characteristics of their ancestors to a dinosaur that has a similar characteristic.

> My great, great grandmother may have been a brontosaurus. She was a tall woman. My great, great grandmother ate a lot of vegetables and salads, too!

Taking It Further . . .

Students can draw their "prehistoric ancestors" or study etymology by writing dinosaur puns.

Subtyrannosuarus Rex (underground dinosaur)
Aereosaur (flying dinosaur)
Tripedosaur (three-footed dinosaur)

Ralph's Secret

Ralph spends a summer vacation with his eccentric Aunt Georgiana and is swept into a wild, explosive adventure with a giant sea monster. Ralph's resourcefulness helps him take care of the monster, his aunt's cooking, and his music lessons in one blow.

New York: Dial, 1983

Weapon

RESEARCH

Materials:

•lined paper
•pencils
•encyclopedias and other reference material

Lesson Procedure

1. Have students work in groups of 4–6 to research different "monsters," such as the Loch Ness monster, Bigfoot, mermaids, or dragons. Using the research information, each team should develop ten questions about their monster.
2. After teams have researched their "monsters," they can challenge each other in a game called "$20,000 Under the Sea." Each team asks a question about one of the monsters.
3. The team that is first able to give the correct answer wins $1,000. If no team is able to answer the question, the questioning team receives the $1,000.
4. The game continues until one team has $20,000 (twenty points).

Taking It Further . . .

Invite students to design their own monsters. Give prizes for the best looking, funniest, meanest, most unusual, or most believable.

Ralph's Secret Weapon

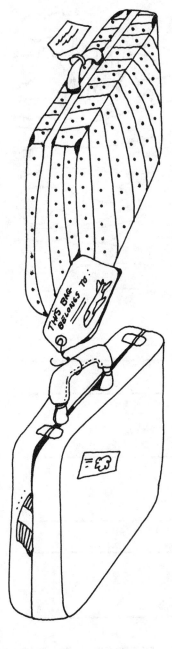

Materials:

•worksheet on page 104
•pencils

Lesson Procedure

1. This is a good activity to do at the beginning of the school year or after students return from a vacation.
2. After reading the story, have students sit in a circle. Ask questions that challenge students to think about experiences they have had that are similar to Ralph's.

   Does anyone have a crazy relative like Aunt Georgiana?
   Has anyone ever had to do something you didn't want to do, such as take music lessons?
   Has anyone ever had to eat something made from a disastrous recipe?
   What are your favorite summer (or vacation) activities?

3. When students return to their seats, have them complete the worksheet with information about their summer or most recent vacation.

Taking It Further . . .

Encourage students to use information from their worksheets to write stories about a fictitious character on an adventure.

Name _____

My Vacation

Someone I visited . . .

_____

_____

Something awful I had to eat . . .

_____

Something I didn't want to do . . .

_____

_____

Some place I went . . .

_____

_____

Something exciting . . .

_____

_____

_____

The Steven Kellogg Connection © 1990 Fearon Teacher Aids

Ralph's Secret Weapon

Tallyho,

Pinkerton's frolicsome mischief goes to the woods. What starts out to be a peaceful picnic turns into a frenetic fox hunt in another madcap adventure with the popular Great Dane.

New York: Dial, 1982

Pinkerton!

Materials:

- light bulbs
- liquid starch
- newspaper
- colored tissue paper
- egg cartons
- yarn
- paint

Lesson Procedure

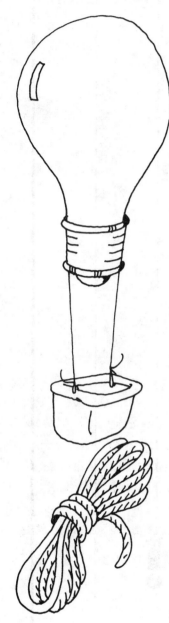

1. Have each student cover a light bulb with several layers of newspaper strips soaked in liquid starch. Allow time for each layer to dry. (The layers need to dry overnight, so the project will take several days.)
2. Students can add strips of starch-soaked colored tissue over the newspaper layers.
3. Have students dip the yarn strips in starch and add them to the light bulbs. The yarn should hang down from the light bulb, so that a basket can be attached.
4. Each student can paint one section of an egg carton and attach it to the yarn strings to make a basket.
5. Hang the finished balloons around the classroom.

Taking It Further . . .

Students can write about their own imaginary hot-air balloon adventures.

Tallyho, Pinkerton!

❧• PLANTS AND ANIMALS •❧

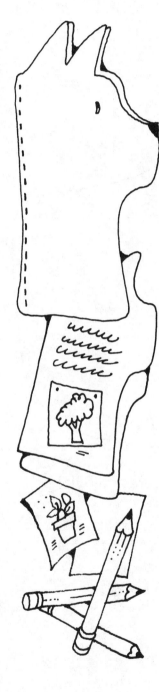

Materials:

- •Pinkerton pattern on page 108
- •unlined paper
- •pencils
- •8 ¹/₂" x 11" construction paper
- •scissors
- •markers
- •stapler

Lesson Procedure

1. Have each student make a booklet by stapling four sheets of unlined paper between two sheets of construction paper.
2. Each student can trace the Pinkerton pattern on the front cover of the booklet and then cut it out to give the booklet the shape of a dog.
3. Have students write "Pinkerton Detective Agency, Plant and Animal Locaters" and their names on the front covers.
4. Students are to locate and identify ten different animals and ten different trees and plants found in their neighborhoods during the next week.
5. Have students draw a picture of each specimen and label it in their Pinkerton detective booklets.

Taking It Further . . .

Use the information in the students' notebooks to make a graph showing which plants and animals are most common in your community. Or, assign individual research projects that use the information students discovered in their searches.

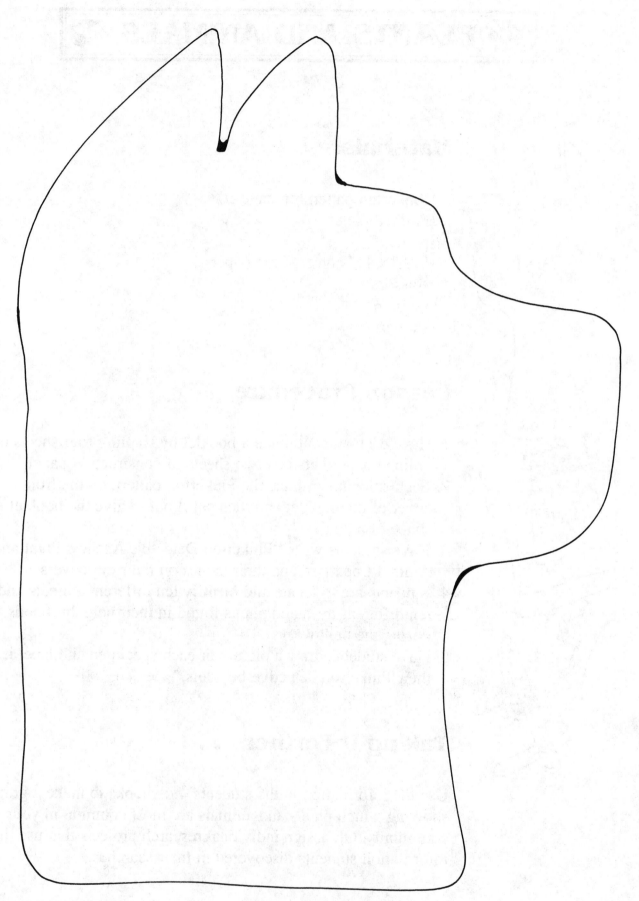

Uproar

Things begin to go wrong from the very start and everyone feels like punching someone in the eye. But family love and effort save an otherwise disastrous day.

Written by Jean Marzollo
New York: Dial, 1982

on Hollercat Hill

❧ • GETTING ALONG • ❧

Materials:

None

Lesson Procedure

1. Discuss things that went wrong in the story.

   The drumsticks broke.
   The train knocked the tunnel down.
   The tractor crashed into the neighbor's car.

2. Discuss things in the story that helped change the mood to a more positive outlook.

   the sun
   tea and cookies
   laughter
   goodnight kiss

3. Ask students to tell about things that have been going wrong for them today.

4. Discuss ways your students can make the day more positive.

   Notice the good things in nature.
   Do nice things together.
   Laugh.
   Show that they care about each other.

Taking It Further . . .

Have students use the worksheet on page 111 to write about conflicts they have had and how they dealt with them. Read *Alexander and the Terrible, Horrible, No Good, Very Bad Day* by Judith Viorst. New York: Atheneum, 1972.

Name _____

The UPROAR started when . . .

_____
_____
_____
_____

The SUN came out when . . .

_____
_____
_____
_____
_____
_____
_____
_____
_____
_____